Here Comes Hortense!

Heather Hartt-Sussman

Illustrated by Georgia Graham

TUNDRA BOOKS

Published in Canada by Tundra Books,
75 Sherbourne Street, Toronto, Ontario M5A 2P9

Published in the United States by Tundra Books of Northern New York,
P.O. Box 1030, Plattsburgh, New York 12901

Library of Congress Control Number: 2011923286

Design: Jennifer Lum
Printed and bound in China

Library and Archives Canada Cataloguing in Publication

Hartt-Sussman, Heather
        Here comes Hortense! / Heather Hartt-Sussman ; illustrated by
Georgia Graham.

ISBN 978-1-77049-221-9

        I. Graham, Georgia, 1959- II. Title.

PS8615.A757H47 2012   jC813'.6   C2011-901385-1

We acknowledge the financial support of the Government of Canada through
the Book Publishing Industry Development Program (BPIDP) and that of the
Government of Ontario through the Ontario Media Development Corporation's
Ontario Book Initiative. We further acknowledge the support of the Canada
Council for the Arts and the Ontario Arts Council for our publishing program.

 ONTARIO ARTS COUNCIL
CONSEIL DES ARTS DE L'ONTARIO

Medium: chalk pastels and chalk pastel pencils on sanded paper and on cold
press illustration board

1 2 3 4 5 6   17 16 15 14 13 12

Nana isn't frightened of the things most grandmas are afraid of.

She isn't scared of spiders or heights. She isn't afraid of the dark or other people's opinions. And, today, in the van on the way to WonderWorld, Nana even takes the wheel because her husband, Bob, sometimes gets a little nervous driving on the highway.

"Maybe, this year, you'll try the Wild Mouse," says Nana.

"Maybe," I say. (I prefer to stay on the Teacups, but I don't want to disappoint her.)

"How about you and I go for a ride in the Tunnel of Love?" Bob asks Nana, squeezing her hand.

"Gross,"
I say.

And Nana and Bob and I laugh out loud.

When we get to WonderWorld, Nana and Bob tell me they have a big surprise for me.

"I thought our trip to WonderWorld was the surprise," I say.

"There's more," says Bob.

"More?" I say.

"It's going to be the best surprise ever!" says Nana.

Just then Bob shouts out: "Over here, honey!"

A gangly girl, about my age, runs over and gives Bob a huge hug. He twirls her round and round.

"Here's your surprise," says Nana. *"Ta-da!"*

"This is my granddaughter, Hortense," says Bob, huffing and puffing and all out of breath.

I knew Bob had a granddaughter, but I thought she lived far away.

"Nice to meet you . . ." I say hesitantly.

"Hey," she says, in an offhanded way.

Hortense can't wait to get our bags into our rooms so she can go on all the scary-sounding rides. She wants to try the Storm Chaser, the Olympian, the Mix Master, and the Wonder Whirl. Then, she says, she'll ride the Flying Carpet, the Landslide, the Flume, and finish the day in the Haunted House and the Hall of Mirrors. She has it all planned out.

I am **nervous** just listening to her.

"What's the rush?" says Bob. "First, let's drop the bags in our rooms."

"It'll be us girls together," says Nana, putting her arm around Hortense. "And the boys can bunk up next door."

I am disappointed. I was looking forward to bunking with Nana. I thought she'd read me my favorite story, rub my head, and sing me "Lavender's Blue."

This is turning out to be the worst surprise **ever!**

Back at the park, Hortense doesn't waste a single second. "Let's go on the Wild Mouse," she says to Nana. "The Teacups are boring!"

"That's the spirit," says Nana, as she skips with Hortense from one ride to the next.

Bob and I try a few, but mostly
we wait on the bench.

Nana and Hortense sure look like
they are having the best time!

At lunch, Hortense grabs the seat beside Nana before I can even get to it. Nana cuts Hortense's grilled cheese sandwich into quarters, like she usually does for me.

"You were right, Gramps," says Hortense. "Nans sure is cool!"

Nans? She already has a special name for my nana?

"Aren't you hungry, dear?" asks Nana, as I stare at my
chicken fingers. Somewhere along the way, I lost my appetite.

Later, when Nana gets cotton candy in her hair, Hortense rushes to help her get it out. She holds Nana's hand all the way through the Hall of Mirrors and even grabs the front row in the Haunted-House mobile, leaving me and Bob to sit in the back.

We can't see anything!

At the ringtoss, Nana wins one of the biggest prizes after just a
couple of tosses. It's a fat pink bunny.

"You don't want this one, do you, dear?" she says to me, handing
it to Hortense before I can even reply.

"I'll get you that giraffe, buddy," Bob says.

It's almost like we're on teams now. But Bob misses. When I try,
I miss too. Hortense howls with laughter, until Bob gives her a look.

Then it's Hortense's turn. Sure enough, she wins the giraffe! When Bob tells her she has to share, she hands me the fat pink bunny.

The worst surprise ever is getting **even worse!**

A t night, when we are all in bed, the walls are so thin, I can hear Nana singing "Lavender's Blue" to Hortense. I know Bob would sing it to me if I asked him to, but he's already snoring.

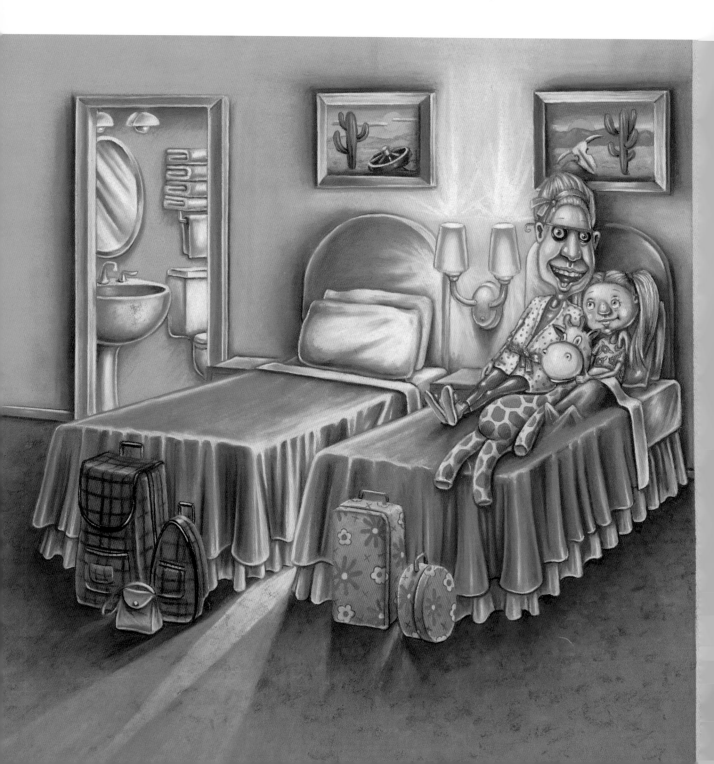

My heart sinks into my belly. I feel a huge lump in my throat.
And I don't end up sleeping very well.

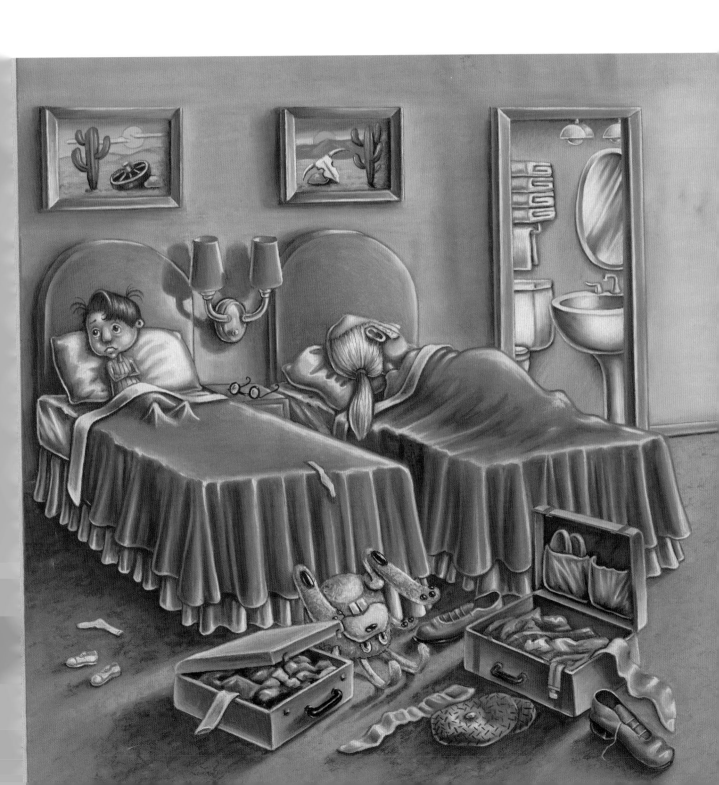

The next day, Hortense is raring to go back to WonderWorld.

This time, she wants to try the scariest ride of them all – the Extreme Flying Machine!

"I'm in!" says Nana, and they give each other a high five.

Bob says he prefers to stay closer to the ground, and so do I. "Looks like it's just you and me again, Bob," I sigh.

"Tell you what," says Bob, putting his arm around my shoulder. "Why don't you call me Gramps?"

"Sure," I say with a smile. **"Gramps."**

When Nana and Hortense return, Gramps says it's finally time for him and Nana to take a ride in the Tunnel of Love. They tell us to wait for them by the exit.

Hortense gives me the cold shoulder.

"I don't know what you have to be upset about," I tell her. "You've had Nana all to yourself this whole trip."

"Well, you've had Gramps!" she shouts. "And I came all this way just to be with him!"

I **never** thought about that!

"What happened to your grandma?" I ask.

"She and Gramps got divorced before I was born," says Hortense. "What about your grandpa?"

"He died when I was small," I say.

We look at each other.

When they come out of the Tunnel of Love, Gramps is holding Nana close. She has her head on his shoulder and is looking up at him with starry eyes.

"They sure look like two happy lovebirds," I say.

"Gross!"

Hortense shouts, and everyone laughs.

When we get ready to leave,
I hand Hortense the pink bunny.
   "Share?" I say.
   "Share!" she says, handing me
the giraffe.
   As we say good-bye, I tell
Hortense I think it would be great
if she could visit us sometime.
   "I'd like that," she says.
We give each other a high five.
   Nana and Gramps smile.

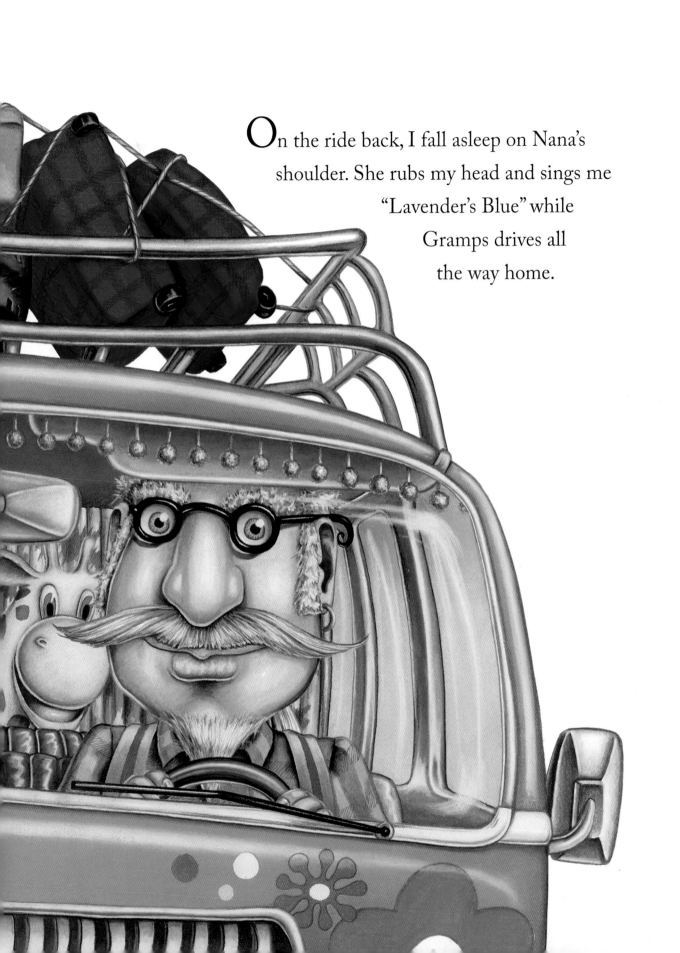

On the ride back, I fall asleep on Nana's shoulder. She rubs my head and sings me "Lavender's Blue" while Gramps drives all the way home.